The Hook Shot

Flairs and Glairs
Publication House

"The Hook Shot"

ISBN No: " 978-93-90416-84-4"
1st Edition
Language – English and Hindi

Flairs and Glairs
Publication House
Regd. Under MSME Act.

Disclaimer

Cover Designing
Shubham Shah

Acknowledgement

Dear Almighty, thank you for blessing me with the power and zeal to be able to complete this Anthology. Also, Thank You dear parents, for trusting in me, and letting me work whenever I wanted. My family is the one who supported me for what I am today.
When it comes to this Anthology, I would like to start with Thanking the Co-authors, without your help and support, I would have never been able to complete it.

Thank You all of you, for being there. Much Love to all of You. I am glad to see you all standing by me.

Co Authors

1. Shubham Shah (Founder Flairs and Glairs)
2. Ishani Agarwal (Co Founder Flairs and Glairs)
3. Shivangi Jaiswal (Compiler)
4. Nishiket R Surwade
5. Priyanshu Somkuwar
6. Ayesha Rajpal
7. Deepjyoti Chowdhury
8. Sukrutha B
9. Atul Kumar
10. Avi Srivastava
11. Ujjwal Shree
12. Lalitha Srinivas
13. Bickey Mandal
14. Grishma Nayak
15. Shobha Rajpal
16. अनिल विश्वकर्मा
17. Vishal Agrawal
18. Prachi Gupta
19. Amarnath Telsang
20. Abhilash Sharma
21. Vikash Kumar Bhakat
22. Arju Mali
23. Ashutosh Kumar
24. Gautam Kumar
25. Prakash Sharma
26. Chirag L Sagar
27. Sachin Banoudhiya
28. Lokesh Upadhyay
29. Faij Ahmad

30. Khushbu Rathore
31. Adarsh Kumar Priyadarshi
32. Pragyan Panda
33. Pradeep Pathak
34. Shajeela Shamreen
35. Reshmi Vernekar
36. Astha Yadav
37. Hema Kirthiga J
38. Sahina Ghugha
39. Sanoj Kumar
40. Aditya Srivastava
41. Kalamkaar
42. Siya Golani
43. Sanya Khanna
44. Yashraj Gupta
45. Vedika Agarwal
46. Sunil Kimidi
47. Akash Goswami
48. S.Prakash
49. Debanjana Ghatak
50. Dr Rakesh R Mund
51. Ajay Poddar 'Anmol
52. Shivansh Sharma
53. Sahaj Sabharwal

Shubham Shah

(Founder- Flairs and Glairs)

Shubham Shah, entrepreneur at “Flairs & Glairs” a brand with dynamics in events organizing and cultural educational pan INDIA, He is a 26yr. old guy who recently has entered, the digital platform of imprinting emotions. He has initiated with his own open mic platform to help budding poets and aspiring writers under his brand named as “Teekhe Zasbaaat”
He is a commerce graduate from Bhagalpur City of Bihar.
He says Writing has impersonated him since childhood and he has now been writing for over a decade!
Cooking, on the other hand, is his passion! He also mentions, trying out new things just tickles him!

When asked sir, Why SPICY EMOTIONS?
He smiled and added, "agar jasbaat teekhe na ho toh wo jasbaat kaha" Spices are all that blends! So do his words!
As a chef, he presents to you his dish! Hot and freshly served! Taste it! Feel it! Enjoy it! You can also find his writing in the Solo book "Teekhe Zasbaaat" and 70+ anthologies. With his passion to explore opportunities across Platforms he is working with keen devotion and We wish him all the very best for his future ventures
Share your reviews on his

INSTAGRAM
@spicy_emotions
@shubham4shah
Or via email on
shubham2shah@gmail.com

To stay tuned to his work and opportunities follow his business Handles

INSTAGRAM FACEBOOK YOUTUBE

@flairsandglairs
@teekhezasbaaat

WEBSITE:
https://flairsandglairs.in/
https://flairsandglairs.com/

Ishani Agarwal

(Co Founder- Flairs and Glairs)

Ishani Agarwal
Born and brought up in Kolkata, she has done her schooling and college from here itself. She is doing her post-graduation at the moment. Ishani loves talking to people around, and is excited for this new beginning of hers! Been a Compiler for 35+ Anthologies, and in the process for more, also, co-authored in 100+ Anthologies, Ishani is very Happy with how her life is turning out now!
Insta handle: Ishani_agarwal_quotes

Shivangi Jaiswal

(Compiler)

Shivangi Jaiswal is a Content Writer from Kolkata. Project Head & Coordinator at “Flairs & Glairs” brand with dynamics in events organizing and cultural educational pan INDIA. Organiser at "The Glittering Fables" Writing Community. She is a B.Com Honours graduate. Certified in Stocks & Short Selling as well as Certified in Digital Marketing Been a keen student, she has recently been Certified for learning Spanish Language..She loves to bring smiles and happiness to many faces, so she is into social service. Shivangi has also done her Diploma in painting, drawing and all kinds of clay making, craft works. Traveler, Teacher, Meditator, Dancer, Singer, Instrument Player. She loves to play guitar and harmonium. Been a public speaker she has taken part in many events and nailed it. Also been a great Advisor to many. Sports freak of Swimming and Badminton with a passion so strong. Since, past one year she has started her writing journey. She writes so that many people can connect with their stories and get positive hopes. She thinks " Every story is unique so embrace yourself to the best".She is a writer by day and a reader by night. Been a Complier of 20+ Anthologies, and in process for more, also Co- authored 80+ anthologies. Shivangi is an old soul with young eyes, a vintage heart, and a beautiful mind."

You can follow her work:

Instagram

@the_knockingvibe

@house_of_compilations

IPL Season Is Here….

IPL Season is here,
The only thing that all people in every city, society craves for it to come.

All teams dealing with excellence.
Whose aim is just one thing "Either Do or Die".

Cricketer's approaching on the ground,
which make us prouder.

The finishing ball, to century hit.
Leaders cheering in the field.

Record of six, six and sixes
That shows the identity of a King,
the Ruler Ruling the field.

And the most awaited part
the IPL Trophy,
which is the prestigious of all.

The brave ones heading up high walking.
Camera's videos, Click! Click! Click!

Blowing buzz
IPL is life of All.

Nishiket R Surwade

Mr.Nishiket R Surwade,born on 24th july 1999 .He is a student pursuing his engineering in electronics and telecommunication field ,Nashik, Maharashtra.He is very shy and simple, easily make friends.He is a blogger and future E&TC engineer.He aspires to become IAS Officer.He started writing as a career since he was in 12th std.He loves to write quote and shayri in Hindi as well as in english language.He loves to write about 'True love' He worked as co-author in some anthologies like 'The Broken Bond','For the name of love' and in more than 25 Anthologies. and also Being a compiler of the book "College Romance" ,"Life Sahi Hai" and many are in process

IPL

IPL ye sirf ek league nahi hai
Isse croro logo ke jazbaat jude hain
Yaha koi aamchi mumbai ka deewana hai
Koi yaha chennai ka fan hai.
Har ek alag team uske aur hazaron chahne wale.
Ye sirf ek league nahi
Isse caroro logo ke jazbaat jude hai

Jab wo match main shuruat hona
Aur apne favourite batsman ko dekhna
Alg tarah ka emotion attachment hai.
Jab wo out ho jaye apne dost se kehna abhi
Match baki hai mere dost
Ye sirf ek league nahi
Isse caroro logo ke jazbaat jude hai

Wo aakhri ki 5 over main match ka
Kaha se kaha pahonch jana
Wo har ball par six aur fours ke barsat hona
Wo hindi main commentary sunna
Ye feeling bass IPL fan samjh sakte hai
Isliye ye sirf ek league nahi
Isse caroro logo ke jazbaat jude hai

(2)

Lakhon ke khwab pura krne ke liye
Ab do sitare humse dur ho gaye hai
Apni batting se dahad te the jo har waqt
Ab wo sher jangle main ruth gaye hai.....

(3)

Corona ne kar diya hai
Haal hamara behal ,
Issi waqt hamare chehro pe
Phirse wapas aa gaye gai India ka tyohar...

Priyanshu Somkuwar

Here is Priyanshu Somkuwar from Nagpur, he is currently perceiving his graduation in Electrical engineering and started holding pen since from his first year. He has been a part of 5+ anthologies as a Co-author. His ambition is to become an IES Officer. He is passionate about writing and expressing his feelings into words.

IPL- The Fan Moment

Saal mein ek baar aata hai ye
tyyohar,
Jhum uthate hai ye log bina kisi
mausam lagta hai sabhi teams
banaygi abhi mahool awsm.

Pata hi nahi hota kab baji palat jaayegi
Palda kiska bhari ho jayga,
Kon trophy Jeet ke apne shahar le jaayegi.

Khele bhalehi ye log ek dusre
ke opposition mein
phir bhi jhalkti hai muskan inke
chehre pe apne pan wali.

Hat's off hai unn sabhi player's ko
Jo banate hai in dino hamara mood,
sahi mein thak jaate honge meters
bhi gin gin ke sixes ke altitudes.

Ayesha Rajpal

Ayesha Rajpal is writer by passion. She is into Nobel profession of teaching and runs an academy in Delhi. She is fun loving and easy going person and has been co author for few books . She is into writing poems . Even she loves calligraphy and Mandala art too.

IPL Hero

Virat ne mara chakka
Sbka dil hua halka
Delhi walon ki jaan
RCB h humari aan baan aur shaan

Jb tum ate ho maza ajata hai
Virat ke balle pr hath lgate hi
Sara mahual garam ho jata hai
Delhi walon ki jaan
RCB h humari aan baan aur shaan

Deepjyoti Chowdhury

Deepjyoti Chowdhury embraces reading and writing as her escape from the real world as well as a window to it. She is a strong believer of Christ and Karma. Written in 100+ anthologies, she is the author of "Heartfelt musings" and "The staircase to freedom". Her main aim is to heal people and make them smile through her art of writing. You can follow her on Instagram at dj_writes_to_heal .

My Captain

The blissful moment when I discovered,
That watching cricket I secretly preferred.

Being from a school where Dhoni had studied,
Where pride and amaze the students bleed.

The Captain had always made me proud,
And removed every questioning doubt.

Being from a small town was now a bliss,
As great heights can be achieved with practice.

Ranchi is now known to all nation,
Because of a single soul full of passion.

Cricket and IPL I no longer miss,
As watching my star fills my heart with bliss.

Sukrutha B

She's an unconditional extrovert and an updating retrograde.
She has a zeal to heal and deal.
A writer with words as double edged swords.
A forever learner with a hope as a rope to cope up with.
Her scope is the stethoscope well she's a doctor to be.

Spirit in The Sport:

Cricket:
It's not a mere theme it's a team;
It's not national it's international;
It's not only emotional but it's more exciting;
It's not about loss but it's all about winning.
It's an emotional entity embedded in the soul.

Win or lose:
You try it's all that thrills;
You coordinate it's all that gives us chills;
You hit it's all that makes us happy;
You catch it's all that makes us caught up with the game.
It's all about a bat and ball with people that makes it a blast.

A game:
An entity of emotion;
An entity of nation;
An entity of union;
An entity of reunion.
It's a spirit and soul to a sport that makes it more special.

Atul Kumar

He is Atul Kumar .He is from Vaishali District of Bihar .He is the student of Delhi University .His favorite game is cricket.

Importance Of IPL To Their Fan

IPL is like a festival for fan .
They celebrate each and every run .
For them last ball finish is fun .

Fan of IPL are unique.
The ran from office early like they going to miss the train .
Fours and sixes make them entertain .

Match by match they support their favorite team .
They support their team like a 12th man .
They support IPL to their TRP Gain .

Avi Srivastava

He is an engineering student aimed to make his name in computer world..
Poetry is not only his hobby but also a way to express his feelings....

क्रिकेट

है खेल ये अनोखा, करता हैं राज़ करोड़ो दिलो पर....
बच्चे बूढ़े हो या हो जवान, हर कोई मरता हैं इस पर.......
हैं खिलाड़ी कई महान, कर रहे रोशन नाम देश का....
करते हैं बारिश रिकार्ड्स की, हो मैदान देश या विदेश का....

देते हैं लोगो को शिक्षा, सिर्फ इंजीनियर-डॉक्टर बनना ही सफलता नही...
सफलता आपके कदम चूमेगी, जो होंगे आपके इरादे सही....
कई लम्हे हैं ऐसे इसमे, जिसको पूरे देश ने हैं जिया.....
ये सिर्फ एक खेल नही, इसने हर दिल को एक किया....

मुंबई इंडियंस.....

जब हुई शुरुआत आईपीएल की, था मैं बहत छोटा....
सबकी तरह खेलने की, ज़िद्द कर मैं खूब रोता....
हमे न थी परवाह उस वक़्त, कोन किस टीम से खेल रहा....
बस देखना ये रहता था हमको, कौन सचिन का छक्का झेल रहा.....

एक वही वजह थी हम सब की, जो इस खेल में बसती हमारी जान....
सचिन की बैटिंग देखने को, हम हर वक़्त रहते हैं परेशान....
बस अब इस वजह से करते हैं, हम इस टीम को सपोर्ट....
बस चाहते हैं अपनी टीम जीते, चाहे सामने कितने भी अच्छे खिलाड़ी हो इम्पोर्ट....

Ujjwal Shree

Ujjwal shree with her pen name Neha Gupta is from Patna, Bihar

She is an avid writer, poetess, and artist. She loves to play with words and write from the depth of her heart. She always express her emotions through words rather than saying. She generally writes about Motivation, emotions, pain and abstract. Writing helps her to survive in her worst phase of life. Writing is just like breathing to her because when she feels depressed she used to write her feelings.

Follow her on Instagram : @Shree22349

Email Id : ng223494@gmail.com

Whoever Wins Love Prevails!

His jersey was red !!
Hers yellow !!

Every six, every four, every run, every wicket was celebrated
Like their teams, she roars like a lioness and he was aggressive....
Everytime she cheered, he smiled at her sheepishly!
Everytime he pumped his fist in air , she pouted !!

One won the match
But they both celebrated the victory..!!
And she smiled, saying "Divided by teams"
He continued, "United by love"

Lalitha Srinivas

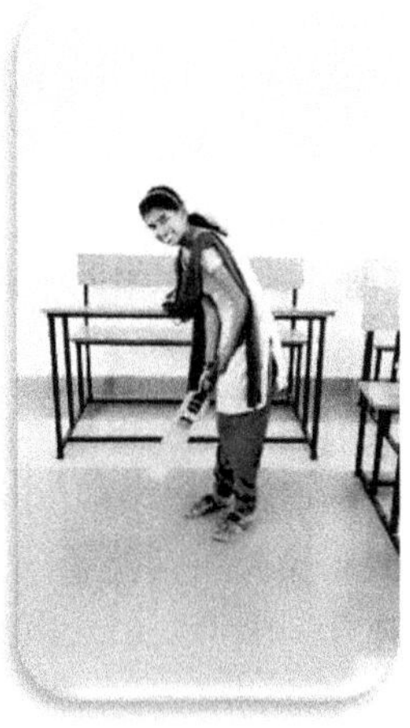

Lalitha Srinivas, born in Andhra Pradesh on 29-11-1994. She has a Bachelor's degree in Computer Science from Jawaharlal Nehru Technological University. She has been part of many anthologies as a co-author. Books she been as a co-author set 2 National record and 2 world records. She is a home maker, attune to create a beautiful art, either it's with ink filled in pen on a paper or brush dipped in paint on a canvas. She is a traveller, who wish to explore the beauty of INDIA, rejoice different cultures and different cuisines. She started writing in her page at Instagram and dedicate it to her late friend who committed suicide. She is inspiring people by interacting with them and understanding their pains, who are in verge of committing suicide. Whenever you feel alone, ping her on.

Insta I'd: @celebrate_golden_days.
Or
Mail: @srijaan4111@gmail.com

Indian Premiere League

The Indian Premiere League.
It is just not a cricket match.
It's an emotion of cores of people.
IPL is the prestigious league of cricket,
Which makes every country play for India.
Each team is the combination of
different players from different countries.
Who represents 8 different states of India.
Proud moment is win or lose,
it's our country's pride to display togetherness.
Most beautiful thing is the players,
Who combat with each other in world cup.
Now play together with joy and spirit to win,
On the name of Indian Premiere League.

Love MI

Dear Mumbai Indians,

I'm a cricket fan. More than anything I'm an IPL fan of your team Mumbai Indians. When I heard the title MI it seems to be similar to my heart. Many people ran behind many teams, but from the beginning I stood by you. You're the first team to win 100 IPL matches. You're the first team who set record of winning IPL for 4 times. Most importantly the brand value of Mumbai Indians is $115 million dollars roughly makes me feel proud to cheer for you. I still remember my school days, when matches are to be held at afternoon. I usually makes an excuse of being sick to bunk my classes and watch your match. I never bother about winning and losing, till end I support you.
Thanking you

Yours faithfully
Lalitha Srinivas

Bickey Mandal

He is Bickey Mandal from Jharkhand. Now he is in the last semester of his graduation from B.B.M.K.U Dhanbad with English Honours. With his poetries he trying to connect himself with others. He is passionate about his works because he love what he do. He have a stedy source of motivations that drives him to do his best. He wants to became a writer from last 5 year so, he collect his Thoughts, Poetry and Lyrics from then to make a good book in his both books he presenting many beautiful shayari, Love quotes , Motivational quotes & sad stories. You can contact him through instagram at @bickey_ki_ankahi_baatein

E-mail- bickeymandal91@gmail.com

आईपीएल का जलवा

क्रिकेट चाहे कहीं भी सुरु हुआ हो ,
पर आईपीएल भारत में सुरु हुआ ।
और इसका नशा कुछ ज्यादा ही ।
सर चढ़ के बोलने लगा ।
चाहे कोई भी हो बच्चे, बुड्ढे या महिलाएं,
सबको ये खेल देखना भाने लगा ।
धीरे धीरे सब इसके ही प्रशंशा करने लगे ।
साल भर का इंतजार करने लगे।
बस इस खेल को देखने के लिए ।
इसके प्रशंसकों का जवाब ही नहीं,
ये आपस में ही लड़ जाते है ,
अपने अपने टीम कि बाते करते करते।
सबके कोई ना कोई पसंदीदा खिलाड़ी है ।
और उसका टीम जिसे वो सपोर्ट करते है ।
मेरा पसंदीदा खिलाड़ी धोनी है ।
और मेरा पसंदीदा टीम चेन्नई सुपर किंग्स ।

Grishma Nayak

Grishma Nayak is a budding writer. She is from Odisha. Her dedication is what sets her apart from anybody else. She is a well rounded individual who lives with passion, dedication and grace.

(1)

करोडो़ दिल जिसे इंतजार करता है
उस एहसास का अंत तूम हो ,
बस मेरे और मेरे परिवार कि नहीं
सबके दिलौं का हिस्सा तुम हो ।

वैसे तो हमें पिला रंग पसन्द नहीं
पर उसे पसन्द करने की वजह तूम हो ,
काम के वजह से दूर हुए परिवार को
साथ लाने का ज़रिया तुम हो ।

"जल्दी से शाम क्यों नहीं हो रहा है "
इस सवाल की सच्चाई तुम हो ,
"आज हमारी ही जित होगी "
इस दुआ कि ताबीर तुम हो ।

तुम कोइ और नहीं
सबकी दिल में बसा हुआ ,
हिंदुस्थान का सबसे बड़ा त्यौहार
IPL हो ।

Shobha Rajpal

Shobha Rajpal is writer by passion. Her love for hindi is divine. She feels quite comfortable with hindi rather english as she loves her mother tongue. She is Hindi graduated and teacher by profession.

आईपीएल क्रिकेट फैन

आया आया आईपीएल का जमाना
लाया लाया चौके छक्को का खजाना
हर कोई है आईपीएल का दीवाना
चाहे हो छोटा चाहे बड़ा सो ना जाना
आया आया आईपीएल का जमाना
लाया लाया चौके छक्को का खजाना

अनिल विश्वकर्मा

लेखक को श्री अनिल कुमार विश्वकर्मा के नाम से जाना जाता है, वे देश की राजधानी दिल्ली से सम्बन्ध रखते हैं। उनकी स्नातक की शिक्षा दिल्ली विश्वविद्यालय से हुई है तथा वर्तमान में वे एक प्रतिष्ठित संगठन में कार्यरत हैं। वे एक गम्भीर व ज़िम्मेदार युवक होने के साथ-साथ कर्तव्यनिष्ठ और पारिवारिक व्यक्ति भी हैं। अपने जीवन के दैनिक कार्यों में व्यस्त रहते हुए भी वे अपनी लेखन रुचि को जीवित रखते हैं। अपने स्नातकोत्तर के दौरान ही उनमें लेखन की रुचि उत्पन्न हो गई थी, किंतु इस कला को भौतिक स्वरूप देने में उन्हें कुछ समय लगा। उनके लेखन की प्रेरणा व स्रोत उनकी प्रिय जीवनसंगिनी है। वे थोड़े अल्पभाषी है किंतु कलम के माध्यम से वे अपनी बात कहना जानते हैं। वे अपनी रचनाओं और लेखनी के माध्यम से आप लोगों से जुड़ना चाहते हैं तथा साथ ही साथ यह भी कामना करते हैं कि आप लोगों का प्रोत्साहन व स्नेह भी उन्हें भरपूर मिले क्योंकि वे इस क्षेत्र में अभी नवीन हैं परंतु इस यात्रा में और आगे तक जाने की इच्छा रखते हैं।

Www.instagram.com/anil0287

माही।।

अपने और इस देश के लिए, उसने एक ख्वाब देखा था,
क्रिकेट खेलने का जुनून, हमने उसमें बेहिसाब देखा था,
कुछ अलग कर गुजरने का, जोश और जज्बात देखा था,
प्रतिद्वंदी से हार मान लेना, उसने कभी भी न सीखा था,
अंतिम गेंद में अक्सर, जिसने गेंद को बाउंड्री पार फेंका था,
जब भी वह मैदान में उतरता, छक्का अथवा चौका था,
अपने इस मुकाम को उसने विश्व कप पर लाके रोका था,
इसके लिए अपना सारा अनुभव और श्रम भी झोंका था,
हमेशा यादगार पारियाँ खेली है, जब भी उसपे मौका था,
उसके जैसा क्रिकेटर किसी ने पहले कभी नहीं देखा था।

Vishal Agrawal

He was born and brought up in mathura uttar pradesh. He is engineering student pursuing his bachelor's degree from GLA university mathura. He is multi talented and multi tasker. He likes singing, skeching and writing. he writes to expresses his feeling and emotions on the paper. Sometimes his quotes and shayri inspire and motivate people. He feels that his hardwork is his biggest strength.

He is co-author of 15+ books which also include vajra world record holder anthology.he is compiler of 3 books: The mysterious life, Verses of life and My Country My pride.

ये सिर्फ एक खेल नहीं

ये सिर्फ एक खेल नहीं
ये तो एक त्यौहार है,
ये सिर्फ भारत तक सीमित कहाँ
इसको मनाता पूरा संसार है,

यहाँ इक्के, दुक्को की नहीं
छक्कों, चौकों से बात होती है,
आर. सी. बी. के मैच में
सिर्फ कोहली, डिविलयर्स के रनों की बरसात होती है,

चेन्नई का धोनी
जहाँ कैप्टेन कूल कहलाता है,
वहीं कोलकाता का रसल
आते ही रन बरसाता है,

चहल की फिरकी
राशिद की गूगली भी है यहाँ,
यहाँ खिलाड़ियों में भाईचारा
सभी का सम्मान भी है यहाँ,

Prachi Gupta

Prachi Gupta is a student of BBA pursuing her studies from Allahabad, UP. She loves to write and reading books as she believes, scribbling can heal all the pains inside your heart. As well as, she is fond of travelling, cooking and watching movies.

Beside this, she is a Digital Marketer and a Writer and a Compiler who has participated in many online competition and won some of the achievement for her best write-up. along with this, she is a co-author of many anthologies.

Contact her:- prachigupt0210@gmail.com
Follow her:- @_prachi_gupta_210_
@prachigupta3435

Supporter of Bangalore

Not last time, not today
But one day.

Not won any,
Not assumed by many.

But I perceive...one day,
RCB will win the whole game,
Because bengaluru has that courage.

I support my team, my city,
I believe in virat and his team.

It's not last, I think
It's just a start.

So many matches are left
And my team is all set to win the rest.

Amarnath Telsang

He is Amarnath Telsang, a young writer;
Even google knows him, If you still don't know him it's you, who are not updated yet.
He is mechanical engineering undergraduate .He is not a poet but writer by passion; who writes based on own experiences.
The words used by him are so deep that can easily touch reader's heart. Kindly visit his accounts once atleast.
For more write ups
Insta I'd : @quoted_duniya (quotes page)
@amarnath_telsang2506(personal)

Royal Challengers Bangalore(Rcb)

You may win or loose
You have won our hearts
This is not just a game
It's filled with emotions
People may talk Hell
But it's really heaven
Years may come n go
IPL is a fest
My team is best
RCBian forever

Abhilash Sharma

Abhilash Sharma a 23 year old passionate writer. He belongs to Sonipat , Haryana . He had completed his B.com (voc) recently. He is a enthusiastic person and a sports lover as well .Worked as a co author in about 10+ anthologies inspired by Ishika Arora and Ishani Aggarwal in the field of writing .You can check out his writings on instagram at @_ankahe_alfaaz__

एक प्यारा सा सलाम देश की इन बेटियों के नाम

जिनका रहा बहुत शानदार ये सफ़र ,
कोई बात नहीं अगर ना मिल पाई हमें अपनी डगर ,
इस बार हारें नहीं है हम , पर पहले से निखरे जरूर है ,
अगली बार फिर से आएँगे , अबकी बार
जीत कर ही जाएंगे ,
शेफाली और ऋचा का युवा जोश हो , या हरमन की
कप्तानी में अनुभव का होश ,
पूनम , राधा और राजेश्वरी की पिरकी की तिकड़ी हो ,
या इनके आगे सभी टीमों की पारी जो बिगड़ी हो ,
शिखा की तेजी हो , या जेमी और स्मृति रहती
मैदान पर बिजी हो ,
तानिया की विकेटों के पीछे की कला हो ,
या वेदा देती अपने अनुभव से कप्तान
को सलाह हो ,
दीप्ति का धीरज हो , बाउंड्री रेखा
पर रक्षक रहते हमेशा सजग हो

Vikash Kumar Bhakat

Vikash Kumar Bhakat is a poet, author, novelist, writer, teacher and a social & educational entrepreneur from Shankarda village near Jamshedpur,Jharkhand. The poet is also the President of Vikash Educational & Charitable Trust. He has completed his graduation in English Language & Literature securing first class position. He imparts free English education to the underprivileged students in Janamdih a tribal dominated village under Potka Block of East Singhbhum, Jharkhand

Mumbai Indians

Can win IPL with certainty
None can ignore its potentiality
This team has great quality
Rohit is the skipper of the team
Shining like sun rays
Excellent batting orders
All are great players
I like them a lot
It fascinates a lot
Mumbai Indians
Like all Indians
Team combination
And its concentration
Has great attraction
And firm determination
It will win definitely

Sourabh Tiwari In Mumbai Indians

He can win hearts of all Indians
Born in Jamshedpur
Plays for Mumbai Indians
Hits long shots
Dashing and dynamic
Young batsman
So stylish
And energetic
Inspires us
To be conscious
Great fielder
Hard hitter
Disciplined and determined
Winning can be achieved
Sourabh Tiwari In Mumbai Indians

Arju Mali

She is a student of Bachelor of Arts. She writes with lots of love, emotions and truthfulness. Her writings mostly portray courage and extend motivation. Writing is her passion.

Instagram: @Arju mali25

IPL

Waqt Ke Bure Huee
Kitna waqt Ho Gaya
Bure Ka Har Kissa khatam Ho Gaya
Jb Se IPL Suru Ho Gaya

Har Insaan jo sirf
Corona Ki Hi Bat Krta tha
Ab Vo apni Team Ke Bare
me Batane Lg Gaya
Jb Se Ipl Suru ho Gaya

Har ghar Me Chalne Vala
Yeah Show Ho Gaya
Sab Sath Milkr Dekhe
ESa Mahol Ho Gaya
Jb Se Ipl Suru ho Gaya

Ab Msgs Par Bhi bat sirf
6 Or 4 KI Hoti hain
Sab Kehte Firte Hain Ki
Meri Team Jeeti Hain

Har Gham Har Paresani
ka hal Ho Gaya
Sab Ki Smile ka PasswordHo Gaya
Jb Se Ipl Suru ho Gaya

IPL IPL Na Raha
Sbki Jaan Ho Gaya
IPL Sbki Muskaan Ban Gaya

Ashutosh Kumar

He is a student and enjoys writing.
A die-hard fan of Mahi.

The Whistle Podu

CSK - the yellow fever
My favourite forever

King of IPL and ruler of our heart
They are artists,if cricket is an art

Dhoni's helicopter shot for six
CSK's winning is fix

Faf's magnificient fielding
Changes the inning

Chahar's dot ball
Makes opponent wicket fall

IPL's most consistent team
Win against it is others dream

This team is never out of game
That's why it is having such a great fame

Gautam Kumar

He is Gautam Kumar belongs to a small town i.e Hajipur,Bihar,India .But he lives in patna for the preparation of Jee. His father is a businessman. And his mother is a homemaker. He always thanks his parents, teachers, and friends for what he is now. As he has a great zeal in the engineering field so he is currently even struggling with his journey to be a renowned engineer. He generally do not show interest in the field of literature but due to this great opportunity he decided to write apart from his career.So in this way he is a co-author of an anthology *WHAT YOUTH LIKE*.You can follow him on Instagram (@82gautamkumar.)

Ipl The Passionating Tournament

In the world many people are interested in playing cricket and watching cricket. Indian cricket board(BCCI) Board of Control for Cricket In India organises many tournaments, one of them is IPL. IPL (Indian Premier League)is a very famous and thrilling cricket tournament. IPL lovers enjoy the IPL as a very big festival. In IPL, players come to play this tournament from all around the world. It has created a huge opportunity in the entertainment industry. IPL is the most watched tournament. In IPL there are 8 teams that represent different cities of India. Before IPL matches there an auction is organised where the franchise and the team coaches select the player who will play from their team. One of the interesting things about IPL is that,in one team there should be only 4 foreign players and the other 7 players should be Indian players. In the IPL many young players have the opportunity to show their talent and skills. From matches of IPL, players are selected for higher level matches like national,International matches according to their performance in IPL.Many fans also waits for their favourite player who take retirement from International matches, they want to see them again in the field to play cricket. In IPL many records are broken to make new records. In IPL every ball is a game changing ball. As all cricket lovers are very much interested in watching IPL and enjoy it very much every season.

Prakash Sharma

"लिख देते है हम दिल के अल्फ़ाज़ युही सुबह - शाम
लफ्ज़ है जो गहरे इतने की ये है बस तेरी मोहब्बत के नाम"

Prakash Sharma is a writer, poet, shayar and author. He writes poem, shayari and quotes which are attach with the life, reality, love and motivation. In personal life he is a student of Law and Chartered Accountancy. You can find him at www.penofshayar.blogspot.com.

आईपीएल का त्योहार

खेल के मैदान में,
लोगो की हर जान में,
हर सख्श की जुबान में,
हर घड़ी और हर शान में,
आंधी या फिर तूफान में
घर या हो दुकान में,
मान हो या सम्मान में,
खुसी और गम का यही मेल है,
चाहे बच्चे,बड़े या हो बुजुर्ग कोई,
हर एक इंसान में बसती है जान वही,
भारत का सबसे बड़ा जो त्योहार है,
आईपीएल आगया फिर एक बार है।

क्रिकेट

क्रिकेट सिर्फ एक खेल नही
हर खुशियों का एक मेल है,

रोज़ - रोज़ की चिढ़ - चिढ़ में
मनोरंजन का ये खेल है,

बैठे जब बच्चे, बड़े और घर के सभी
तो सब पिक्चर भी अब फेल है,

ईद कहो या दीवाली कहो
ये त्योहारों जैसा खेल है,

जोश और उत्साह से भरा
हर गम भी अब फेल है,

क्रिकेट सिर्फ एक खेल नही
हर सख्श की ये जान है
देश या फिर विदेश कहो
इस खेल का सम्मान है।

Chirag L Sagar

Chirag L Sagar is a 1st year MBBS student studying at Srinivas Institute of Medical Sciences and Research Centre,Mangalore. His hobbies are poetry, reading - books,novels, autobiographies,philately, listening to songs,sports like cricket and badminton,cooking. He is a medico by profession and a writer by passion. His best friend Nihar,has always been his inspiration and motivation to do great in whatever he does. His dream is to become an Oncologist and a successful writer.

Instagram : @chirag_cls18 Facebook
Chirag LSagar

(1)

For IPL fans, IPL is not a tournament, it's an emotion.

(2)

IPL is a festive season for all cricket lovers, specially for MSD fans.

(3)

IPL is the only point of the year that everyone realizes to work in unity.

Sachin Banoudhiya

He is a student of Bsc
A Struggling Writter now Started Getting so many platforms
He Loves to do Audio Poetries & video Editing .
He's a Publish Co - author in so many Anthologies

Msd Retires

Jise bachpan Se Khelte Dekh
Main Bada Hua Tha
Jise dekh Apne Pairo Par Khada Hua Tha
Started From Zero
Ended Up Being A Hero
From Nothing To Everything
Here's How The Name
Mahendra Singh Dhoni

Jisse dekh Kar cricket ka matlab pata chala tha tha
Aksar Ek Ummed Si rehti Thi
Maahi Hai naa
Wo Dekh Lega
Cricket ka mtlb He Maahi Hota Tha Hamare Liye
Kirdaar Nibhane Wala Kya Chala Gaya Tumne to kirdaar He
Chhod Diya

Bhale Puri Team Haar ki Kagar Par Ho
Ye Ek Banda Oura Game Palate ka Dum Rakhta tha
Zindagi Se Bas Ek Yehi Shikayat Rahegi
Aakhiri baar Tumhe india ke Liye
Fairwell match khelte na dekh paye
Tum bhale He India ke liye na khelo par
Ye Desh Tumhara Aaj bhi Shukragujar Hai
Or hamesha Rahega

Lokesh Upadhyay

Lokesh Upadhyay, resident of buxar district in Bihar, presently he is a student in class 12th Dandi Swami sahajanand saint Vinova college. He has a keen interest in writing his heart out in the form of small poems, porses and verses. He hope you will enjoy reading his work and appreciate it.

Thank you..

मेरी वफायें याद करोगे

मुझ से बिछड़ने के बाद तूने कई लोगो से वादे किए है,
उनके साथ जीने मरने के इरादे किए है,
पर शायद हम दोनों जैसा इश्क़ हर बार न हो,
मेरे जैसा अब कोई तेरा दिलदार न हो,
तेरे बेवफ़ा हो जाने पर भी कोई जान देने को तैयार न हो,
इसलिए कहता हूं तुम उसे कभी झूठे ख्वाब दिखाना मत,
बीच चौराहे पर अपने हाथो से उसे अपनी जूठी मिठाई खिलाना मत,
उसकी जूठी चाय कभी पीकर उसे अपनेपन का एहसास दिलाना मत,
बिन मतलब के 100 वादे उससे कर के मुखर जाना मत,
अपनी बाहों में लेकर उसे कभी जोर से गले लगाना मत,
जिस तरह मुझे ना भूलने की कसमें खाई थी कभी उसके लिए खाना मत,
मेरे माथे पर जो दगाबाजी वाला दाग़ लगाया है कभी उस पर लगाना मत,
मेरे जैसा रोते - बिलखते उसे छोड़ कर जाना मत,
जेसे मुझे तोड़ा, उसे तोड़ कर, बीच राह में मुंह मोड़ कर,
सदा के लिए उसका साथ छोड़ कर,
कभी कहीं जाना मत,
क्यूंकि सब लोकेश नहीं मिलेंगे,
कितना भी नफरत कर लो, हर वक्त बदले में उसके प्यार नहीं मिलेगें,
तुम्हारी हजार बुरी बातों के बाद भी तेरा साथ देने वाले यार नहीं मिलेंगे,

जेसे मुझे बर्बाद कर के गए हो वैसे किसी और को कर जाना मत,
क्यूंकि सब मेरे जेसे ईमानदार नहीं मिलेंगे।

Faij Ahmad

He is Trainee navigational officer cadet at shipping corporation of india. He is a free lance writer. You can connect him on insta @shibbuahmed

Cricket

A big name in itself
Not just a game
But way more than feelings

Indian kids
Before opening eyes
They take their bat first
In Early morning

Comparing themselves
With great players
Wearing tshirt of their name
Like this their day start

They sing,play and celebrate
The language of Cricket
Adding emotions in every sphere
They ball and bat

With spirit of camaraderie
Like brothers
They play and win
Together

Khushbu Rathore

An independent soul who likes to read, write, pants and design. A girl who, through poetry, expresses her feelings and enjoys comfort.
B. Ed is very talented girl with getting education. A proud girl from Pali district of Rajasthan receives her education during the day and most of her time in the night gives her time to the writing work. She is Khusbu Rathore and is delighted to be a part of this anthology
Instagram =@khushburathore1913

आईपीएल का बोलबाला

कभी एक आईपीएल ऐसा भी हो
जिसका खुमार आईपीएल जैसा हो

कभी ऐसी गुगली आए
कि बेरोजगार आउट हो जाए
गरीबी LPW हो
मंहगाई रन आउट हो
भ्रष्टाचार जो लगातार स्कोर कार्ड बढ़ाए जा रहा है
उनका इनसे भी बुरा हाल हो जाए
जब एक लंबी हिट लगाए तो
बाउण्ड्री लाइन पर कैच आउट हो जाए
हमेशा मैच हमारा भारत ही जीते
ग्राउंड चाहे जैसा भी हो

कभी एक आईपीएल ऐसा भी हो
जिसका खुमार आईपीएल जैसा हो

हम सभी हिन्दुस्तानी एक टीम है
हमारा एकता अखंडता में ना कहीं फिक्सिंग हो
दंगों की ना डेड बॉल हो
भेदभाव की ना नोबॉल हो
लिंगभेद करने वालों पर सदा प्रतिबंध लगे
परस्पर प्यार और भाईचारा का मैच हो

Adarsh Kumar Priyadarshi

Adarsh Kumar Priyadarshi is a school going boy form a small town called Hajipur, Bihar. His father servers the nation in Indian Army. And his mother is a housemarker. He is co-author of 40+ anthology As he is proud to be the son of a loyal army man so he too wants to do something great for his mother-land. As he has a great zeal in medical field so he is currently even struggling with his journey to reach his destination, his goal i.e. to be a renowned doctor. He always thanks his parents, teachers, friend and God for what he is now.

His debut, book will be launched soon.

You can follow him on Instagram (@adarsh_priyadarshi_03)

IPL

Yes I love it,
The way it is.
The four and sixes
On the ground.
Which excites the crowd.
The 20-20 format,
The colour jersey
With the sign of a Town (state).
The batting and the fielding
Which make our brain sine.
Yes I love it,
The way it is on the ground.

Pragyan Panda

Pragyan is persuing her B.Tech in "Chemical Engineering" from IGIT, Sarang. She's a short girl from Rourkela, Odisha. With fascination of nature, she's a spiritual person who motivates people. She does weird stuff like interacting with non living ones and pens down her mind. For more of her works, do follow her IG @quote_love_97.

Connecting Crews

A whole of a locality united;
A bunch of status piled:
With argument of heartbeat and completion;
Eight teams initiate the game.

The game of zeal and fire,
Shower of immense glory;
The celebration of India;
Every day with its theory.

The festival got its own charm;
More to entertain the souls scam.
Yes cricket at its best_
IPL matches outdoes the rest.

Pradeep Pathak

Pradeep Pathak a simple boy residing in Bihar and belongs from Nepal. He is currently persuing B.sc. He is a creative writer with full of naughty mind. He always trys to make his ideology unique and that's why his creation looks more striking. He is a published Author and taken part in many anthologies. Indeed he is totally rapt in his own creative world. His work includes~ poetry,microtale,quotes,and lyrics.

Contact him on :
Email : pradeeppathak0604@gmail.com
Instagram - pradeep_ptk
Facebook - Pradeep Pathak
YouTube channel : Poetical pen
Your quote : Pradeep Pathak Vats

Near My Heart

I have seen many sports till now, but my first love is none other than IPL. IPL is not just a game, it is an emotion associated with millions of people, it is the heartbeat of millions of people. Before the IPL starts, we set every date of the match according to our schedule, keeping our TV recharge and sports channels ready for the IPL to be broadcast. Or say that we take care of every little thing with great curiosity. As if nothing is more important than that. And why not, because we are afraid that no match will be missed,No laughing moment disappears from the eyes. We want to capture every scene in our eyes so that we do not ever regret that we lost those thrilling times. In this, we have our own favorite team who play, it seems that we are playing, if they win, then it seems that we have won, and if they lose we also suffer. All of this directly means that we are tied to them through a thread of thought and emotion. In the meantime, do not know how 1-1.5 months pass. But when the IPL season ends, then we get disappointed in our lives. But then a wave arises with a hope in the chest to be ready again for the next year, for a new beginning.
Then there will be a new morning, then a new character, when those happy moments will come, they will definitely come.

Shajeela Shamreen

Shajeela Shamreen is a co author of many anthologies.she is currently pursuing a undergraduate degree in literature.she is on the process of becoming a well defined writer and soon she will achieve it. A strong dreamer basically,who wants to make those dreams true soon.

Indestructible Army

The team with great strength,
courageous and brave
Plays for the state,
Players like warriors
And captain like commander
Takes the privilege of the state
And heads forward
Everyone longs to see them on field
And when they come on field
Watching their batting
Will be like a heaven feel
The team and the captain
Shares the bond
Which is like;
brothers from a same family
Share between them
People waits for them to come
And at last when the time nears
People loses their patience;
At the time when all players
Come on to play
Cheers and voices will be heard over
To see them and their game
Everyone will have a own team,
In their places
But ours is different
It's a emotion,sentiment
Love,happiness,unity
Everything in one together
And it is our Csk Forever!

Reshmi Vernekar

Reshmi Maheshwar vernekar has completed her Master degree in (hindi language) and currently doing bechular degree in education (b.ed) at pragati women's collge of education at torxem she want to become a teacher her hobbies are reading books,cooking, she also like to do social services

भारत का त्योंहार आईपीएल

आ गया भारत का त्योंहार आईपीएल, अब हर कोई अपने टीम के लिये नारे लगायेगा। कोई कहेगा मैं एम आई का फैन, तो कोई कहेगा मै केकेआर का, तो कोई मैं आरआर का। साल के दो महिने सब उठाते है इसका तुफाँ। यंगस्टर को बढ़ावा देता है, यह एक्सपोजिशन टैलेंट का।

लेकिन इस साल हम हमारे माही को याद करेंगे। शाम को ७ बजे से टीवी के सामने बैठकर पिरवार के साथ खेल देखेंगे, हर कोई किसी दुसरे टीम की बुराई करेंगे, जितेंगी भाई जितेंगी अपनी ही टीम जितेंगी कहकर चिडायेंगे।

अपनी टीम का समर्थन करने मैदान तक जाने के लिए खड़े थे डट कर ताकी उनके कदम न कभी लड़खड़ाए, पर क्या करे इस साल हमारे हिंदुस्तान में आईपीएल ना हुयी तो अगले साल मैदान तक जाकर फिर जमकर अपनी टीम को मजबूद बनायेंगें।

टीम की एक विकेट गीरने पर चिढ़ना, और अपनी टीम जीतने पर मन भर कर खुश होना। खेल के आखिरी पल बहुत ही इमोशनल होते है। चेहरे पर दुख का हाव भाव सब एक हो जाता है।

लेकिन मै तो मेरी केकेआर के साथ हूँ लेकिन मेरी दीदि सचिन की फैन होने के कारण एम आई का साथ देती है।

क्रिकेट खेल ही बड़ा रोमांच का खेल है। कब क्या हो जाये किसका भरोसा है। कोई मन ही मन खुश होता है कि उसका फेवरेट खिलाड़ी आज सौ बनाएगा तभी अचानक वो आउट हो जाता है।

क्रिकेट के चक्कर में टीवी सिरयलो का तब बडा नुकसान होता है क्यों की पती और पत्नी के बीच रिमोट के लिए चली नोकझोंक में हमेशा क्रिकेट प्रेमी पती जीत जाता है।

क्या हुआ इस साल स्टेडियम में तालियो का गूँजना नही है। हम घर बैठकर हमारे चहिती टीम को पुरा सपोर्ट कर रहे है।
हर किसी के होंठो पे मुस्कान और आँखों में आरज़ू है। हर कोई अपनी ही टीम जीत जाए यह भगवान से कामना कर रहे है।
क्रिकेट का प्यार ही अजीब होता है। फाइनली कोई भी जीतें, लेकिन आईपीएल देखने का मजा कुछ अलग ही होता है एम आई ओड इयर्स के बादशाह माने जाते है। २०१३, १५, १७, १९ का कप उन्होंने उठाया था लेकिन २०२० में भी पूरी ताकत लगानी है क्यों कि इवन इयर का पन्ना इतिहास के किताब में अभी आना बाकी है।

Astha Yadav

Astha Yadav is from Uttar Pradesh. She's an amateur writer who loves to spill her emotions on the pages of her diary. Astha has participated in more than fifty books as a co-author including record holder books. She has compiled eight books till date. She's a vajra world records holder herself. Her only dream is to make her parents proud and happy.
Insta id- red_rose431

Captain Cool

To our dearest captain cool,

The news of your retirement from International cricket broke lakhs of heart. I remember the time you brought Cricket World Cup to India, that picture is still printed on my heart and I'm sure no cricket fan can ever forget it!

You are humble, down to earth and calm nature has always inspired me. Your patience while playing cricket is visible on television screens. And what is more loved by every cricket fan is your wicket-keeping. There is none who can match your level of wicket-keeping.

The day you announced your retirement from international cricket, we all were eagerly waiting for IPL to start, to see you batting again, to watch your aura and playing cricket again. Now, IPL is the only place where we can watch you playing cricket and your strategies to win match.

You will always be in our hearts forever! Thankyou for giving us countless memories and amazing moments to cherish forever!

With love,
One of your die hard fan.

Hema Kirthiga J

She is Hema Kirthiga J, and her pen name is sparkle. She is professionally a psychologist and passionately a writer. She heals others but writing heals her. She is writer, reader, orator and a believer. She is from Chennai. She lives by the principal of inspire and be inspired. She writes her heart and soul and she deeply believes that the depth of her heart and the nib of her pen are soulfully connected. Writing is an art and she is a proud artist. She loves what she does and loves what she writes. You can reach her at

Instagram- @the_pen_queen
Email- inker.sparkle@gmail.com
Yourquote – JKM

Oh My God!

Closing my eyes!
Peeping through the holes!
Out or not i was worried!
And then he gave me 6!
Oh my god.

Match

Everyone on the sofa!
Eyes on the screen!
Ears on the speaker!
Match brought us together!
The joy!
The tears!
The excitement!

Sahina Ghugha

Sahina Ghugha is 20 year old b.com student at Saurashtra university Rajkot. She is from Jamnagar city of Gujarat. She is state level winner in poetry competition 2017. She is Co-author of 10+ anthologies. She is an amazing writer and poet and she wants do something for society through her pen.

क्रिकेट - एक नशा

क्रिकेट से है कुछ मेरी ऐसी यारी
ये है तो लगे सारी दुनिया प्यारी
भूख प्यास कुछ याद ना आए
जब कभी बात क्रिकेट की आए

सारे खेलो का राजा क्रिकेट कहेलाता
ये हर युवा, हर राज्य को है भाता
"इंडिया का त्योहार" गाना गाता
आईपीएल में हर बच्चा लहराता

बल्ला और गेंद जान है हमारी
इसी पे तो टिकी है खुशियां सारी
लगा लू वर्ल्ड कप में गालो पे तिरंग
देख जिसे दुनिया रहे जाए दंग

Sanoj Kumar

He is an engineer, started writing two years back never imagined that people would like it, and feel his emotions as theirs. He also likes to express other's feelings and always try to change other's mindsets in a better way through his writings. Nowadays he is a member of many writing communities and earned lots of certificates through his writings. His first book as an author is launched from a " poetry world organization " named as " सफ़र, जिन्दगी का ". " Fam-Bond in lockdown " is his first anthology as a compiler and editor while he is a co-author of many anthologies.
You can see his poetry on Instagram @the_hidden_writer_sk
And an article on blogger @http://safarzindagikask.blogspot.com
Contact him through his mail id @thehiddenwritersk@gmail.com

क्रिकेट का रोमांच

फिर शुरुआत होने को है, क्रिकेट का वहीं रोमांच।
जब विरूद्ध होंगे एक दूसरे के, धोनी, कोहली और युवराज।

पल भर में हार से जीत हो जाए, तो छन में मैच का पासा पलट जाए।
कोई विकेट लेने की लड़ी लगाए, तो कोई छक्के का बौछार कर जाए।

एक महीनों का है ये त्योहार, ना कोई देश ना कोई विश्व का वार।
जो ना भी हो क्रिकेट प्रेमी, वो भी हो जाते, मैच देखने को तैयार।

रोमांच का हर सीमा पार कर दे, हर मैच में कोई नया रिकॉर्ड जड़ दे।
ऐसा ही है ये खेल आईपीएल का, क्रिकेट प्रेमी में नई ऊर्जा भर दे।

Aditya Srivastava

Aditya is a future engineer. He had also been part a of 10+ anthologies and writes when he desires to.He wants to make his career in research field and wants to find something great for the good cause of the world. You can connect to him at: @b.e.z.u.b.a.n__d.i.l

(1)

Aasman me helicopter dekhu toh tu yaad aata h
Kahi kisi ko peeli jersy me dekhu toh tu hi nazar aata h

Tu batsman
Tu captain cool
Tu best finisher .
.
Tere bina har match begana lagta h

(2)

ग़म के अंधेरों में खुशियों का अंबार आया है,
सूने नुक्कड़ों मे हाको का बौछार आया है
शोरो से गूंज रही गलियारे, जो कल तक गुमसुम थे
यह आईपीएल का रंग है, आजकल पूरी दुनिया पर छाया है।

Kalamkaar

This is kalamkaar. He is from uttrakhand but broughtup in Meerut (Up). His hobbies are reading and writing. He love writing. He is part of 200+ anthologies as co- Author. He won 150+certificate in writing. His interest is in writing. He is simple and people observer.

महेंद्र सिंह धोनी

रांची का एक मध्य वर्ग का लड़का
खेलता था फुटबॉल और था गोलकीपर
बाइक का वो दीवान था
दिया क्रिकेट के कोच सर ने चांस उसको तब बना वो विकेटकीपर
आने के लिए क्रिकेट मे लगाई अपनी रेलवे की नौकरी दाव पर
आया फिर क्रिकेट की दुनिया मे नया सितारा
क्रिकेट फिर लगा उसको सबसे प्यारा था, खेलने दोस्तों के संग जाता था
चलता बल्ला उसका सबसे न्यारा
शार्ट वो ऐसे खेलता बॉलर भी डरजाते
डाले कोनसी बोल उसको पूछने कप्तान के पासजाते
डाले अगर योर्कर तो हेलीकाप्टर शार्ट घूमजाता
बॉल फिर सीदा आसमान को चूम के आता
बुरी परिस्थिति मे भी करता नहीं था कोई भी भूल,कहते थे उसको कप्तान कूल
क्रिकेट का वो है नायब सितारा, जिसकी वजा से टी 20 और विशव कप हुआ था हमारा
दिलाये कही ख़िताब उसने करा परचम भारत का ऊपर
अनहोनी को भी जो होनी कर देता था
नाम था उसका महेंद्र सिंह धोनी

Siya Golani

Siya golani is a creative writer. She has inclination to positive aspects of life. She is a confident presenter who keeps her views very subtle but firmly. She evokes her messages and effectively engages the audience through her writeups.

Its A Six

OMG! Six, wow what a move.this is usually my language in this IPL season. The favorite time of the year. It is a ritual to hold popcorn in one hand and T. V remote in other and shouting what a shot, well done. All are my favorite teams every time i see a cricket match i feel energetic and enthusiastic.

My heart beats faster all the time when the bat hits the ball. I keep aside all the work and sit infront of the T. V and shout yaayyy.

Sanya Khanna

Sanya is someone who always manages to create a positive aura around her. She is constantly smiling without complaining much about the difficulties. She is confident in whatever she does and is very hardworking. She has never learnt to give up in life. Whatever the situation maybe, she completes all the tasks given to her on time and in an organised manner. She has a keen interest in writing and feels that she can express herself truly through her words. She manages to work well in a team.

"Our Love for The Game"

The IPL season has begun,
A spark is ignited into everyone
Each day sharp at seven,
We sit in front of our television..

Be it Bangalore or Rajasthan Royals,
We are the fans who are always loyal
Not to a team, but towards the game
We never watch it just for the fame!

Our love for cricket is paramount,
The number of runs is just an amount..
Nothing can define our passion for the game,
Some call it obsession, some call it lame!

Cricket teaches us an important drill,
It's okay to be aggressive or a little chill
And it's never an individual but the team
That helps one shine like a beam!

Yashraj Gupta

Yashraj gupta,son of Mr. Vivek and Mrs.Aarti gupta,is only 10 year old budding writer.He is recently in class 4. He loves to write poems and songs. He has an ability to engage his readers through his writing.Apart from this he loves to play cricket also.

"आइ.पी.एल फीवर"

आइ.पी.एल के फैन बड़े,
चर्चे इसके हर रोज़ चले,
दुनिया भर में जाना जाता,
ये खेल बड़ा पहचाना जाता।

मनोरंजन का साधन बना,

आइ.पी.एल बड़ा लोकप्रिय बना,
जन-जन के मन को भाता आइ.पी.एल,
घर में झगड़ा बढ़ाता आइ.पी.एल,
सबकी नींद उड़ाता आइ.पी.एल,

सबको मज़े दिलाता आइ.पी.एल,

कोविड में दिल बहलाए आइ.पी.एल,
सबके मन को भाए आइ.पी.एल,
घर-घर इसी की चर्चा चले,
आइ.पी.एल के फैन बड़े।।

Vedika Agarwal

She is Vedika Agarwal a student of Bsc home science, Delhi university. She likes to write and draw a sketch. She is passionate for dancing, singing and acting. She is a determined, bold and a kind hearted girl. She is very conducive in nature. She loves to spend her leisure with old age home people and orphanage children. She loves to learn new things. She is a very emotional girl. She loves to help others. She loves to write. She has a very helpful and loving nature towards the people.

Cricket:A Sport Or An Emotion

Remember when we used to play cricket
It's being played in every street or the corner
And we used to make the wicket with the help of bricks
And then decide the rules of the game
If it goes out of a boundary then 6 and if it goes inside the house then it will considered out.

First ball used to be the trial ball for every player
No run for wide balls
It was so much fun

This created a passion in the hearts of people for watching these cricket matches
The IPL match is the one where total 8 teams used to play
In this all players got mixed up in every team
Which represents unity, no discrimination only brotherhood.

This is the only match I have ever seen from my childhood the most
I enjoyed playing it with friends in my childhood time
Now I enjoyed seeing my favorite players playing match on the field

I too love to watch cricket matches
Which also teaches a person the importance of teamwork and cooperation
IPL make people learn to live a life with patience

It is the only game which has made the people fans in each and every corner of the world
Even busy people take out time from their busy schedule to enjoy these matches
In India people used to wait for these IPL and for other cricket matches.

I too love cricket which I can't even express
My favorite team is CSK at the time of IPL
For which I eagerly wait for their match
It was a great moment to see all the players together on the field
Sitting at home we feel like we are in the fields and expresses our joys, happiness, cheering up them, and when any of the player gets out then to be a little sad
These are the days when mostly family used to watch matches together.

Sunil Kimidi

Sunil Kimidi named person was gifted to this world by Ramu & Mani on 1995/12/24. He worked as CAD engineer in Visakhapatnam. He wrote many quotes about his Life partner, Parents and Family members. His contents are full of patriotism and respect for women. The essence in his writings attracts everyone.

Just as there are many stars unseen in the sky, so many beautiful feelings that we do not see are hidden in his heart.

"Perfect entertainer- IPL"

No matter how much burden we bear throughout the day, we get relief once the match starts. I think that there is no other medicine can heal us as the way Ipl does. Ipl fans renamed summer as Ipl season. We don't care our problems while watching matches. During Ipl season we can have an excellent sleep for sure. Because we generally involve in the matches irrespective of the team and players. Our tiredness from the day time's hard work simply disappears. Even old people can enjoy the match and simply addict until the last match. We generally enjoy our favorite hero's film until few days after release of the movie. But we enjoy the entire ipl season without any drop outs.

"Happy faces"

When we see the fours and sixes, we feel as if we are standing on the crease in the places of actual batsman. Our legs never stops dancing even after the match ends. We share more hugs with others without our knowledge. We order special food for having stuff. After completion of ipl season our faces turns dim as if we lost someone. That's the greatness of Ipl.

Akash Goswami

Mr. Akash writes poems, phrases which considering where you're reading this, makes perfect sense. He is an excellent writer who speak through his pen, His every writing has a backstory. He is fluent in his native language , Hindi. He mainly consider this language for writing his poems.

॥ अब फैंस बोलेगा ॥

कोई सिर्फ़ खेल कहता है।
कोई अवसर बताता है,
मगर क्रिकेट की दुनिया में!
इसे सब "मनोरंजन का बाप" समझता हैं।

IPL युवाओं के भविष्य की सीढ़ी है।
इससे वंचित हमारी कई पीढ़ी है।
हौसला जुटा कर बदलते रहे है फ़ैसले,
ना रूके थे और ना रूके है कभी।
आसमाँ में मार कर है डुबकी,
क्या खूब बजवाते है फैंस से सीटी।

खेल जमाते है, वापस जीतने का क़सम भी खाते है।
यूँ ही नहीं, भारत का एक बड़ा त्योहार बन जातें है।
गेंद का धागा खोल, जब बल्लेबाज़ गर्दा उड़ाते है।
यूँ ही नहीं, सुपर ओवर हम फैंस के साँसें अटका जाते है।

जहाँ हुनर से चिरते है खिलाड़ी अवसर के परदे,
जहाँ लगते है विश्व भर के रणबाँकुरे के मेले,
जहाँ लोगों के हुजूम से बौने लगते है स्टेडियम,
चमकने के लिए इसलिए मोहताज नहीं है
आईपीएल का रेडियम ।

नज़रों में हमारे जज़्बा वही रहेगा,
खेल परखने का तजुर्बा वही रहेगा,

ऐसा मौक़ा और कहाँ मिलेगा?
IPL का संग्राम हमेशा चलता रहेगा ॥

S.Prakash

Prakash is actually a man of love. The one who was born to give lots of love, care and affection to fellow people in this universe and cherish them with unbound love. He is fond of spending alone time letting himself to discover his innerself. He is having a unquenchable thirst towards writing that always wants him to let his thoughts to reach an unimaginative extent of this universe. He is very much interested in doing creative things rather than following a track laid by others. He is not a rule breaker biut not a follower too. He might not have great achievements in life, but having a innumerable potent seeds to sow in the beautiful garden of his life. He is pursuing his dreams and pushing his efforts towards a epitome of greatness.

Never Give Up On Dreams

Sports teaches you that there is always a second innings in life. If you fail today, there's a second innings maybe two days later.

When you die, leave no dream left behind.
Leave no opportunity left behind.
When you leave this earth, accomplish every
single thing you could accomplish.
You're gonna be a hero one day, but you will never get here.if you give up, If you give in, IF you quit, you finally gotta wanna succeed as bad as you wanna breathe..

Enjoy the game and chase your dreams. Dreams do come true...!

(2)

Cricket wanted the world to feel more like a book: Here is a question, so here is an answer. Here are the mysteries of the universe; now here is everything you want to know about them

We get so used to playing in favorable conditions, that we fail to realize that the ball has started moving but our feet aren't.
The conditions become favorable by adapting to them, and adapting means being open to change in the technique & temperament.

Think of yourself as an cricketer. I guarantee you it will change the way you walk, the way you work, and the decisions you make about leadership, teamwork, and success.

Debanjana Ghatak

Debanjana is a simple girl and down to earth by nature. By profession she is an English Faculty at a reputed Educational Institution. She is an ardent lover of Nature, animals, Literature and a believer of God. She loves to dream and enjoy dwelling in her fairy tale land. She loves to enjoy the tiny rays of happiness hidden in the smallest moments of life. In short she describes herself as a dreamer and believer. Whenever she felt the presence and beauty of love and got smell of Nature, a new poetry or a story took birth. She believes in the philosophy of never giving up. She doesn't give up dreaming and believing in what she believes.

Dear Captain

I was never a cricket fan rather I used to hate this game and considered it as the most boring game of the world. I often asked dad that why did he watch cricket so dedicatedly. He smiled every time. One day in late 90's, I was just a little kid then heard about the glory of Bengal, Sourav Ganguly and he was playing an awesome innings against which team I don't remember now but the match was super exciting and thus cricket won a fan that day which is me.

Now, it is controversial that I started loving cricket for the sake of the game or for my fondness towards Ganguly. Yes, I am a great fan of Sourav Ganguly and I believe he is the best captain of India to date. Why? Because it was he, who went to the World Cup Final, 2003 with eleven new and inexperienced cricketers. Although India lost the match but it was a good fight. He is fearless and has a leadership quality. I respect him because he is genuine and has a never giving up spirit which inspires me the most.

He has ruled and played a major part in my childhood days. I even wished to be a cricketer but my parents stopped me to see such dreams. Every evening after school my friends and I used to play cricket and that made me happy and confident. Now I am busy thus I can't play but my love and respect for Sourav Ganguly is alive in my heart and I am proud to see him as the President of BCCI.

Dr Rakesh R Mund

Dr Rakesh R Mund has been participating in more than 70 anthology and his solo books are ishq-e-panhi & Vidhwansh available on amazon, flifpkart and others platform. He read veda and diffrent literatures which give a glimpse on his writing. You can contact with him : insta- Rakeshmundr_

अपराजेय

अलग खुशी होता है दिल में
इश्क़ से कम नहीं,
बटकर अपने ही सितारे रहते
अलग कौई गम नहीं ।
चेन्नई का वो ताज माही अपने
दिलों का सरताज,
जब चल जाऐ हेलीकॉप्टर तब
दिल का वो मोहताज ।।

पिला रंग सर चढ़कर यही बताता
हम किसीसे कम नहीं,
हलके में उसे लेकर कभी भी उसे
हराना किसीमें दम नहीं ।
सुरेश जाडेजा वाटशन् केदार
डु-प्लेसिस संग चावला,
सामने वाले हो जाते इनसे
भिड़कर कभी कभी बावला ।।

ब्राभो ठाकुर चहर रायडू ये भी
कम नहीं किसीसे,
रंग छुडाने संग पिले जर्सी का
जंग नहीं किसीसे ।
अलग पहचान रखकर अपने
प्रशंसक भी अद्वितीय,
ढोल नगाडे बजाकर जब होता

मैदान में अपराजेय नृत्य ।।

Ajay Poddar 'Anmol

He is Ajay Poddar 'Anmol' from kolkata, mainly his most of works started from Uttrakhand he used to live in Madhyapradesh he is the only person in his family who loves literature because he thinks only literature and positive literacy can change the world and society after 7 years of struggle he entered in literature fully by professional development from dream analysis,He want to proof that universal fact literature is directly proportional to science and science is directly proportional to god and god is directly proportional to literature

शीर्षक- उड़ते हुए एहसास

24 लोगों का खेल 15 अंदर लाखों बाहर,
करोड़ों का एहसास है क्रिकेट,
सच कहूं तो जज्बात है क्रिकेट,
सिर्फ खेल नहीं है,
पूरी दुनियां को एक साथ बिठा दे,
वो खयालातों का पहाड़ है क्रिकेट,
धोनी के छक्के गांगुली का रंग,
सहवाग की साझेदारी सचिन के संग,
क्रिकेट ही तो है कुंबले का ढंग,
युवराज के पारी से दुनियां है दंग
नये दौर का नया माहौल,
कोहली के साथ उतरा है रोहित उस ओर,
गंभीर का झटका बॉलर को भी पटका,
क्या भूल गए वो 2 अप्रैल 2011 का शोर?
1985 का विश्वकप जब भारत लेकर आया था,
हर युवा बूढ़े बच्चों में ऊर्जा भरपूर छाया था,
वही कप दुबारा देखो कैप्टन माही लाया था,

क्रिकेट का दौर भी बदला खिलाड़ी भी बदल गए,

पल्लू शॉट से हेलीकॉप्टर तक देख सारे पिघल गए,

आईपीएल के कारण देखो खुशियां फिर छा जाती है,

नीली जर्सी देखो फिर 8 रंग दिखाती है,

एक एक बॉल से भी मनोरंजन करवाती है,

Shivansh Sharma

I am shivansh sharma . Basically from indore but persuing MBA(Marketing &Hr) in mysore karnataka . He always have passion towards writng the thoughts which comes in to his mind . A hardcore fodiee as he belongs to indore . He is the one who is always ready to help to his near ones .His life revolves around his family and friends. He is always self motivated , enthusiastic and person with positive vibes .He is co-author of 10+ books and compiler of 1 book . His oy belief is just live happily and enjoy every moment of life .

You can contact him on ig@shivanshrockzzzzz

माही

पीली जर्सी पहना एक खिलाड़ी था,
क्या बाजी है खेली उसने
किसी अकेले का नहीं ,
पूरे भारत का दिल जीत गया ,
एक नहीं अंगीनत बाजी खेली,
कितने ही 6 मारे कितने हैं 4 मारे ,
कितने आईपीएल मैच है हारे
वो विकेट के पीछे खड़े होकर ,
अंदाज़ - ए- बयान से ,
हर किसी को है लुभाया ,
अपने हर खिलाड़ी को ,
हर बार है समझाया ,
हर बार आखरी तक खड़े होकर ,
मैच जीतने के प्रयास है करे,
आईपीएल में हर मैच के ,
मुश्किल के घड़ी में उसके
चेहरे पर मुस्कान है देखी ,

अपनी मस्ती में खेलते ,

अपनी टीम की कई किताब है जीताए,

हर बार हार के बाद खुदको आगे खड़ा

कर अपनी टीम के खिलाड़ियों का

हौसला है बढ़ाया,

हर जीत में अपने आप को पीछे

कर दूसरों को आगे है करा,

हां वो एक ही था ,

वो कोई और नहीं हमारा मही था ,

वो एक माही तो ही था ,

क्या बाजी खेलकर दूसरों का दिल जीत गया ,

अपने बल्ले ,अपनी कूल कप्तानी से

करतब है दिखाए उसने सबको ,

चंद पलो में खुदने आकर मैच पलट देता था ,

वो माही ही था

Sahaj Sabharwal

Personality Of Jammu, India
Name: Sahaj Sabharwal
He loves writing poems and thoughts. He lives in Jammu city, Jammu and Kashmir, India. His date of birth is 17th March, 2002 . He has been awarded many awards in poem writing at State level, National and international level. He was also selected to be invited for the International Writers Meeting In Tarija And Hungary,Europe. He Was Awarded With The International Diploma In Writing And International Merit Certificate In Writing And Was Published By The Young Writers Association In Uk And Recieved "Certificate Of Publication From Uk". He was also awarded the 'India Star Proud Award'
for his appreciable work and He is the author of the Book -: " Poems By Sahaj Sabharwal "
Contact-: sahajsabharwal12345@gmail.com

महेन्द्र सिंह धोनी

क्रिकेट तो एक ज़रिया था,
देश के लिए इनके दिल में कुछ कर दिखाने का बहता दरिया था।

ये अपने जीवन की समस्याओं से न डरे,
अच्छे से लड़े, तब कहीं जाकर आगे बढ़े।

जितनी देर ये खेले, इन्होंने आराम से अच्छा समय बिताया,
सन् 2011 में इनकी कप्तानी ने भारत को विश्व कप जितिया।

बल्लेबाजी, गेंदबाजी, विकेट कीपिंग आधि सबमें अच्छे थे,
यही नहीं, ये मन के साफ और दिल के बहुत अच्छे थे।

कैप्टन बनकर खिलाड़ियों को अच्छे से खेलना सिखाया,
भारत देश किसी से कम नहीं है, पूरे विश्व को दिखाया।

Flairs and Glairs, a platform by a student for the students. We are esteemed youth struggling to carve out our path for our future and we follow a basic mindset Since everyone is not born with all-round skills. Joining hands with people who are born to execute it with perfection is the best way to evolve. Self-Evolution is the need of the hour but, evolving as a community is what we strive for. The initiative as kickstarted by, Founder- Mr. Shubham Shah with the motive to utilize the skillset and talent of writing has now a team of 10+ people who are actively participating into newer forms of learning and discovering talents among youngsters. We Provide platform and services like Publishing opportunities, Open mics, Workshops, Hands-on training. Operating with Brand Name Of Flairs and Glairs (Publication House), we offer the chance of elevating a passionate writer to an esteemed author With Brand name Teekhe Zasbaaat, We bring to you an opportunity to get accustomed with the Public Speaking and Presenting of Thoughts along with regular challenges to brush up your nking spirit. The newest initiative to extend our services we introduced in a new writing Platform- The Glittering Fables and Ink Over Tears.

We Choose to Fly Like A Falcon than to be a

Leg Pulling Crab.

www.ingramcontent.com/pod-product-compliance
Ingram Content Group UK Ltd.
Pitfield, Milton Keynes, MK11 3LW, UK
UKHW022005190726
13853UKWH00004B/1746